The SHEEP in WOLF'S CLOTHING

HELEN LESTER

Illustrated by LYNN MUNSINGER

SCHOLASTIC INC.

New York Toronto London Auckland Sydney
Mexico City New Delhi Hong Kong Buenos Aires

To my son Jamie,
with thanks for thinking of . . . *Mother.* — *H.L.*

ISBN-13: 978-0-545-15769-8
ISBN-10: 0-545-15769-2

Text copyright © 2007 by Helen Lester.
Illustrations copyright © 2007 by Lynn Munsinger. All rights reserved.
Published by Scholastic Inc., 557 Broadway, New York, NY 10012,
by arrangement with Houghton Mifflin Harcourt Publishing Company.
SCHOLASTIC and associated logos are trademarks and/or
registered trademarks of Scholastic Inc.

12 11 10 9 8 7 6 5 4 3 2 1   9 10 11 12 13 14/0

Printed in the U.S.A.   40

First Scholastic printing, April 2009

The SHEEP in WOLF'S CLOTHING

Ewetopia was not comfortable in her own wool.
She always needed to hide in an outfit, and spent a fortune
on her clothes.
But no one paid any attention.

She attempted to dazzle the rams.
But Rambunctious, Ramshackle, and Ramplestiltskin barely blinked.
She even tried to shock the other ewes.
But Ewecalyptus, Ewetensil, and Heyewe hardly noticed.

This lack of attention annoyed Ewetopia like a bad itch.

Then one fine day she received an invitation to the Woolyones' Costume Ball.

Yes! Here was her chance.

She'd have the finest costume in Pastureland and outshine them all. Every fluffy one. Ha!

In a frenzy of excitement, Ewetopia tried
on fifty-seven costumes. Her clothes-changing
muscles were aching—almost worn out—
when she put on outfit number fifty-eight.

That settled it. This was the one! Ewereka!

She loved the warmth of the fur. The shine of the fangs. And especially the way the long-clawed paws swung attractively when she walked. Everyone would notice her now!

On the eve of the Woolyones' Costume Ball, Ewetopia arrived with her heart aflutter.

She waited for someone to invite her to dance.

And waited. And waited.

And while she waited, the ewes and rams did sheeptrots and waltzes, and gathered in small groups to whisper and point.

"Shhhhh. Bad taste," remarked Ewecalyptus and Ewetensil.

"Shhhhh. Faulty judgment," added Heyewe.

"Shhhhh. One wonders what sort of family she comes from," wondered Rambunctious and Ramshackle.

"Shhhhh. Cotton-brained idea!" pronounced Ramplestiltskin.

Then all of a sudden as the sheep waltzed and whispered and
Ewetopia waited, a stranger entered the ballroom. A handsome
stranger, a charming sheepish grin, and wool so lovely,
it looked fake.

The sheep were so taken with the beauty of this creature, none
stopped to wonder why a sheep would go to a costume ball dressed
as a . . . *sheep*.

The flock gawked.

Ewetopia approached the stranger.
The stranger approached Ewetopia.
From under his sheep costume the newcomer could
see the fur, the fangs, and the long, sharp claws.
It had to be.

In a low, growly voice he exclaimed, "MOTHER!"
Mother? Beneath her costume, Ewetopia blinked.
Mother? She knitted her eyebrows (a sheep thing).
"Mother," growled the creature, "I thought you
were away on a lamb hunt."
Lamb hunt?

Ewetopia found this puzzling, but she did
need a partner, and so their dance began.

"Ah, Mother, Mother," the stranger growled in one ear.
"I've missed your home cooking," he growled in the other ear.
"Especially the ewe stew with ram ramen."

Then he growled in both ears,
"Let us grab a couple of fat woolyones, leave this silly ball,
go home, and dine on sheep."

Ewetopia sensed that something was wrong.
Dine on sheep? What kind of a creep would dine on a sheep?

For the first time Ewetopia noticed her ex-partner's long, sharp claws and extremely hairy feet.

And then it hit her.

She had not been dancing with a sheep dressed as a sheep at all.

Oh, no. She had been dancing with a real *wolf.* Big, bad, and mistaking her for his mother!

This varmint posed a danger not only to her but to all those in the ballroom.

Indeed he did, for just then he ripped off his
costume and growled, "Come on, Mother. Let's eat!"
With that he snatched Ewecalyptus, Ewetensil, and Heyewe
and stuffed them into a sack.

The woolyones gasped in horror
and ran for their lives.

What to do?

No time for wooly-brained thoughts.
Ewetopia paced in circles.
Mother . . . mother . . . mother . . .
He thinks I'm his mother!

Then she stood up as straight as she could in her foolish
costume, lowered her voice to a growl, and announced,
"Sonny dearest, I have a surprise for you."

"Surprise!" growled the wolf. He loved surprises and would have squealed with delight, but wolves aren't good at squealing. Ewetopia needed to stall for time, as she hadn't the foggiest idea what the surprise might be. So she tried to think of motherly things to say.

"First, my son, before the surprise you must take a *bath,*
clean your *claws,* and brush your *fangs.*"

The wolf moaned, "Aw, Maaaaaaa."
"After that you must do your homework. All of it."
The wolf whined, "Mommmmmeeeeee."

"Then, sonny boy, you *must* pick up your room."
That did it.

He threw himself onto the floor and into a full-blown, out-of-control tantrum.

"I WON'T! I WON'T!" He kicked his feet.

"YOU CAN'T MAKE ME!" He pounded his furry fists.

"I DON'T HAVE TO, SO THERE SO THERE SO THERE!"

So great was his tantrum that within less than a minute he was completely exhausted and unable to move.

It was then that Ewetopia knew what the surprise would be.

She flipped off her furry costume, bent over the helpless wolf, and announced,

"Surprise! I'm a ewe!"

The wolf opened one eye. "You're not a me. I'm a me. You're a you."

"That's what I said." Ewetopia smiled. "I'm a ewe."

"Who's a who?" The wolf was flustered.

And Ewetopia repeated, "I'm a ewe."

This was too much for the wolf's small brain to process. Muttering "I'm not a you. You're a you. I'm a me. I came in as a me, and I'll leave as a me," he dragged his weary self to the door, forgetting all about dinner.

He paused and gave one last howl:

"And I'll never ever EVER pick up my room!"

With a stomp and a thomp, he was gone.
Ewecalyptus, Ewetensil, and Heyewe
scrambled out of the sack and hugged
Ewetopia.

Everyone in the ballroom sang out, "What kind of a creep would dine on a sheep?"

For the rest of the evening Ewetopia had a ball.

She danced with Ewecalyptus, and Rambunctious, and Ewetensil, and Ramshackle, and Heyewe, and Ramplestiltskin.
And she felt entirely comfortable in her own wool.